JAMES STEVENSON

THAT DREADFUL DAY

GREENWILLOW BOOKS NEW YORK

10 9 8 7 6 5 4 3 2 1

Library of Congress
Cataloging in Publication Data

Stevenson, James, (date)
That dreadful day.
Summary:
When Mary Ann and Louie
return unhappily from
their first day at school,
Grandpa tells them
about his own dreadful
first day at school.
[1. Schools—Fiction]
I. Title.
PZ7.S84748Tf   1985
[E]   84-4164
ISBN 0-688-04035-7
ISBN 0-688-04036-5 (lib. bdg.)

"On that dreadful day,
I got up very early so
I'd be right on time.

There was a drizzle and dense fog.

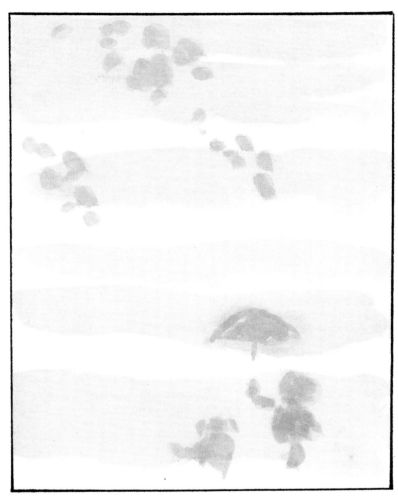

I walked and walked, but
I couldn't find the school.

"Somewhere the school bell was ringing. It made a dismal sound."

"It looked ghastly.

"Suddenly a girl ran out the door."

"I looked inside. The room
was huge and dim and still.

"As I walked through the door, something grabbed me!"

"I was put in the back of the room."

"We watched Mr. Smeal go running down the road. He got smaller and smaller, and was never seen again.

The next day we had a new teacher who was very, very nice!"